W9-CSJ-067

DANCING HEART

An Indian
Classical
Dance
Recital

DANCING HEART: AN INDIAN CLASSICAL RECITAL

Published by Shanti Arts Publishing
Shanti Arts LLC, Brunswick, Maine 04011
www.shantiarts.com

Printed in the United States of America

LCCN: 2016932101

ISBN: 978-1-941830-77-2 (print; hardcover)
ISBN: 978-1-941830-31-4 (print; softcover)
ISBN: 978-1-941830-78-9 (digital)

Dedicated to Sahebru (Lakshman).
May his love for Thillana live on.

ACKNOWLEDGMENTS

Rani Iyer is grateful for the support and encouragement received from many Bharathanatyam Gurus over the years. She is especially grateful to her mother for introducing her to this form, though she quickly realized that writing is more her mettle than dancing. Visit her at www.raniyer.com.

IMAGE CREDITS

front cover, Rajesh Narayanan/Shutterstock.com; back cover, Jack.Q./Shutterstock.com; pages 1, 11, Rajesh Narayanan/Shutterstock.com; 2–3, dwphotos/Shutterstock.com; 4–5, Veranika Alferava/Shutterstock.com; 6, 15, 30, 31, Jack.Q/Shutterstock.com; 6–7, 14–15 background, Tania Anisimova; 7, freya-photographer/Shutterstock.com; 8, 14, f9photos/Shutterstock.com; 9, Ashwin/Shutterstock.com; 10, f9photos/Shutterstock.com; 12, 13, 16, 17, 19, 21, 22, 23, 24, 27, Rajesh Narayanan/Shutterstock.com; 16, 17, 28, 29, Snezh/Shutterstock.com; 18, Shymko Svitlana/Shutterstock.com

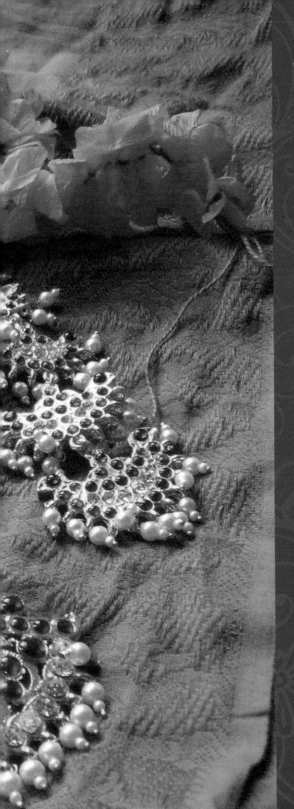

Welcome to an Indian dance recital!

Here, you will feel the rhythm.
Dimmi Thakka
You will hear the vocals.
Gaaaw jaaaw Naaaa Naaaah
You will see splashes of color and movement
Swish, Swish

The artiste or dancer you are about
to watch has learned the art from a
guru or teacher for seven years or
more. In this dance, each body part
is useful, every gesture is purposeful.

The dancer synchronizes them
to tell the story of life.

Enter the auditorium now!

Natyam, the dance, needs a song for rhythm.
When a dancer has sufficient training to keep
the gestures, emotion, expression, and movement
in sync with the rhythm, they can almost dance
anywhere and to anything.

Thàllàngu-thàkàjànu!

Thàkkà-dimmi!

Thàkkà-Jànu!

Thàm-thidthàm!

Thyai-di thyai!

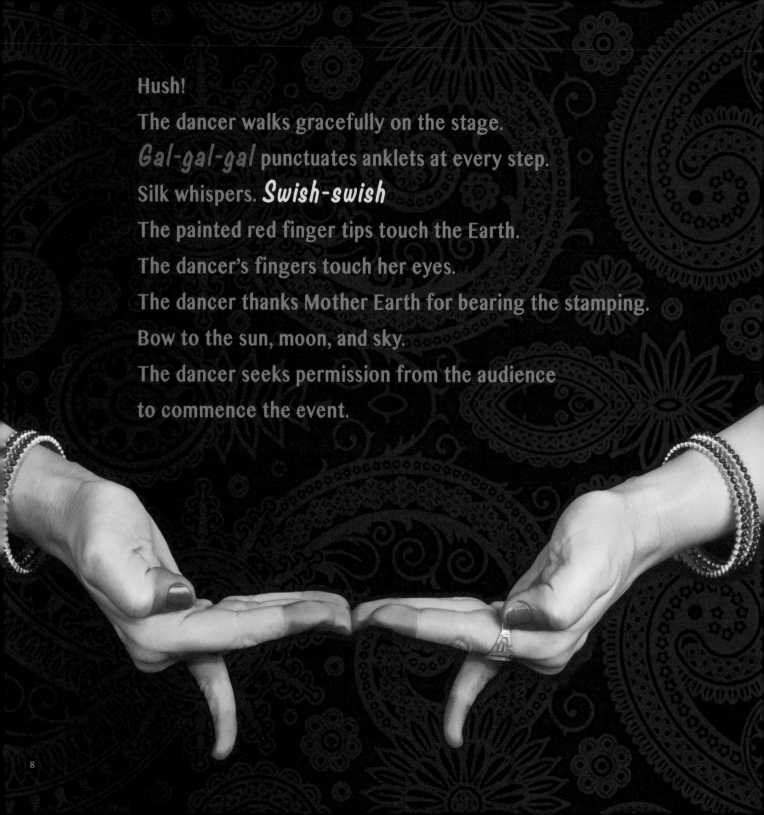

Hush!

The dancer walks gracefully on the stage.

Gal-gal-gal punctuates anklets at every step.

Silk whispers. **Swish-swish**

The painted red finger tips touch the Earth.

The dancer's fingers touch her eyes.

The dancer thanks Mother Earth for bearing the stamping.

Bow to the sun, moon, and sky.

The dancer seeks permission from the audience
to commence the event.

The flower-filled palms shower respect to all.
Ting-jing-jing ...The petals ...f.. l ..o.. a.. t...
The dancer moves like a taut bow. *Gal-gal-gal*
Gàà-jàà-nààà-nààààààààà
The sharp vocals wrap the audience.

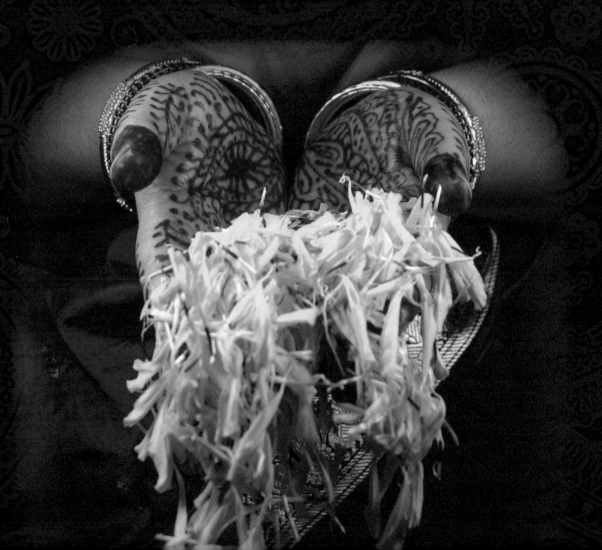

The cymbals clang. *Ting-teing-ting*
The dancer bows and enters the spotlight.

Click-click-whirl

Cameras flash!
The audience settles down with a sigh.

11

Like a flower blossoming in stages,
the beats —

Thom-theay

— and gestures are
woven together.

Thikattaka-thom

12

The beats gradually become faster.

An accordion-like fan on the dance dress opens and shuts as the dancer moves.

Dazzle! Dazzle!

Golden and bright!

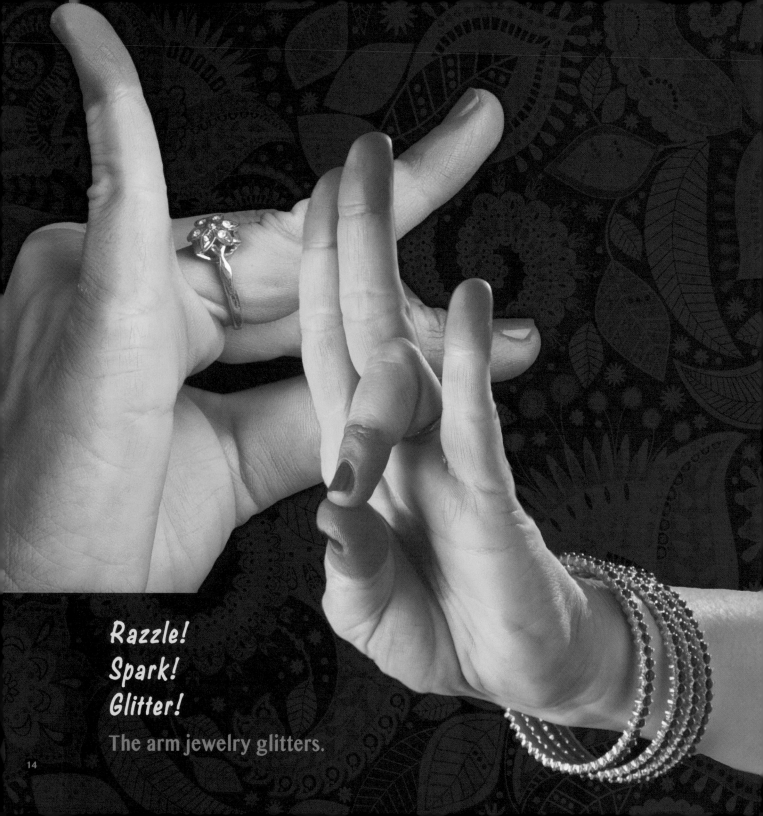

Razzle!
Spark!
Glitter!

The arm jewelry glitters.

14

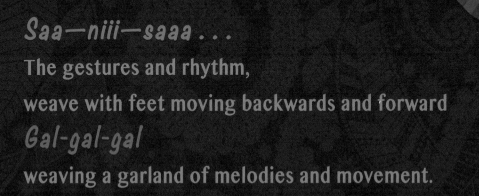

Saa—niii—saaa . . .
The gestures and rhythm,
weave with feet moving backwards and forward
Gal-gal-gal
weaving a garland of melodies and movement.

The melody
Aa — aaa — aaaaa
swells inviting the
gentle movement
with the beats.

Thaais— Tattha — Tham
The dancer's face crumples,
shoulders slump,
a slouching walk.
Oh! The sadness.

The audience
watches the
dancer's
emotions.

Gal-gal-gal

An excited
jump.
A careful
tread.
The story shows
a feeling.

Razzle! Wink! Dazzle!

A feast for eyes.

A pleasure for the ears.

Hearts burgeon with every note.

Another mood is painted by the dancer.

Oh! That naughty child!

Catch him! Hold him!

Come here . . . Stealing butter are you?

Shattering pots . . .

Thud! Crash! Thud!

These tiny, milk soaked footprints . . . oh!

The dancer speaks the story with the melody

Kannaaaaa . . . vaaa . . .

in grace and movement .

Many ways, of using melody,
 to tell an incident to a friend . . .
Saaaa . . . Kkkhiii . . . Yaeeee . . .

He swaggers, she sways . . . a friend laughs . . .
tell me more she says . . .
Gal-gal-gal and giggles . . .
Swish swish and **Cling-clang** of bangles
The audience is at the edge of their seats.

What is the secret in this dance story?

Vocals stretch. *ya . . . aa . . . ae . . . ee*
Cymbals clang. *Thi . . . Thi . . . Thi*

Oh! The girls!
Their dancing whispers are all about a
crush . . . a love.

Thadana—dheem—thadana—dheem...
goes the melody.
The footwork is
brisk and rigorous...

Gal...gal...gal...
gallagala...gal

Leg extensions...dazzle..dazzle...
Thadana— dheem—dheem
in diagonals and circles.

Stillness for seconds as the cymbals beat . . .

Thi . . . thi . . . thi . . .

out-turned feet, bent knees, and erect torso . . .

The tempo quickens. The dancer whirls.

And as the last beat echoes, the dancer stands still

Like a temple statue.

A breathing sculpture
with a dancing heart!

Cosmos, Earth, and everything that sustains life . . .
Gratitude . . . palms folded and bending forward . . .

May peace prevail everywhere!
For all times.
For every creature!

Ting! Ting! Gal—gal—gal!

The audience erupts!
Clap! CLAP! CLAP! CLAP!

The dancer bows.
With eyes, arms and graceful movements
A story came to life . . .
Just for you!

About Bharatha Natyam

The dance style described in this book is one of the classical dances of India called Bharatha Natyam (Bhaa-RaaDha-Naatyum). It originated in Tamil Nadu, a state in southern India. An old style of this dance used to be performed at temples. Boys and girls, men and women can perform the dance. Those who wish to learn the dance must study under a guru or teacher, and must practice more than two hours daily.

Bharatha Natyam consists of pure movement (Nritta-Nurttta), expression of emotion (Nritya-Nree-thea), and drama or portrayal of character (Natya- Nat-yah). A balance of all three of these characteristics is required in a dance performance. The technical aspects of the dance are described below:

Pages 4-5
The debut of a new artiste is called Arangatrem (literally means entering the stage).

Pages 6-7
Bharatha Natyam, has Bhavam (bHaa-Vhum) — expression, Ragam (Raa-ghum)— melody, and Natyam (Knat-Yham) — portrayal. A dancer teams up with musicians to present the narration.

Pages 8-9
Flower offering is called Pushpanjali (Phu-spha-anjaylee).

Pages 10-11
The dancer bows to the cosmic dancer and to the audience before beginning any performance.

Pages 12-13
Just like the flower blossoms, so does the movement in the sequence called Alarippu (AlAr-iPhu).

sequence is called Jathiswaram (jeTHEEsworoum).

Pages 16-17
In Sabdha (Shhabdha), an emotion as well as dance is added to the sequence.

Pages 18-19
The coloring/acting of the piece by the artiste is called Varnam (Wharnum). This is the longest part of any recital.

Pages 20-21
Padam (Padhum) is a Natyam piece and portrays a character, including emotions.

Pages 22-23
Usually, Ashtapadi (Ash-tha-padhi) describes devotional compositions on Krishna.

Pages 24-25
Thillana (Till-anna) is a piece with complicated movements and postures. It is usually performed at the end of the recital.

Pages 26-27
Thillana also incorporates rapid movement and stillness combined with rhythm and silence creating a memorable experience.

Pages 28-29
Mangalam (Mung-alam) brings peace for all beings on earth.

CPSIA information can be obtained at www.ICGtesting.com
Printed in the USA
LVIW01n2116080516
487278LV00006B/11